TILL THE EDGE OF DOOM

VISHNU

I dedicate this work to almighty.

Contents

Preface

Firstly, Thanks for your valuable time. This is my first published work albeit I have written some short stories and poems. The idea of the story and the title " Till the edge of doom" inspired from William Shakespeare's Sonnet 116 which remains the grammar of love till the edge of doom. This is a fictional love story. The idea sparked my mind during global lockdown due to COVID pandemic. I hope this story will keep you engaging. Thanks again.

Prologue

This is a fictional story of two lovely souls, Sita and Vasu. Lets go through this wonderful love journey.

ONE

FLOOD OF REMEMBRANCE

It was a delightful dawn, the best time for the official merger of two secretly merged hearts. The wedding hall was filled with fun filled families and friends. The old man arrived late, while the ceremony was going on. Seated at the last bench, he was in the flood of remembrance.

It was a 9.15AM at Chennai in India. The fully loaded sub-urban train was waiting for green signal as rabbit waited for tortoise. One of the daily passengers was Vasu. He was working as a software analyst. Born in a middle class family, he lived a life with minimal things. He had more liabilities than assets. The prices of everything got inflated except his salary. Though he had a bus facility which took few minutes to reach his office, he opted train which tours the whole city to reach the destination. All these adventures in daily journey was meant only for saving 50 rupees. He believed his difficulties would end up only when he would go abroad. He had been looking for the vacancy in foreign branches. He had been waiting like an owl waiting for a night time, the right time.

Sita, a fresher seeking for a job, came Chennai from her native. She had excellent oration skill. Even an introvert would become extrovert while talking with her. She had attended many interviews but got knocked out in the very initial stage due to lack of aptitude solving skills.

TWO

THE FIRST MEET AND BUDDING LOVE

One Friday, Sita came to attend the interview in the same office where Vasu worked. Vasu greeted all the candidates and gave instructions since the manager was arriving late. Sita like every other time got rejected in aptitude test. She got vexed and sat down for a while keeping her file aside. After few minutes, she went from the office with misery. She didn't realise her file missing.

On evening, When Vasu was leaving the office, he saw the file on table. He found that it was the file of one of the applicants. He noted her mobile number and residential address. He was surprised to see as Sita was residing in the same area where Vasu lived. He took the file with him. On the same day night, after reaching home, he called her and told that her file was with him. Then only she realised it. He also told her that he was living in the same area. He asked for a meeting the next day in a nearby park. She agreed.

The nextday, being a holiday, the park was full of crowd. Vasu was waiting for Sita. She came. She thanked for safely handing over the file. She started asking him about any job openings. Thus, the conversation started. Within minutes, they were talking like they knew each other for ages. She told him about her aptitude weakness and asked whether he could help him. He agreed to help her.

Both met frequently. Gradually She skilled in solving aptitude. Vasu developed feelings towards her. Finally, she cleared an interview and got a job. She thanked him. He felt happy for her. Vasu started writing his feelings and affection in his diary. But he never revealed it. Though he got an offer to work in London, he kept it pending .

THREE

SUFFERING OF TWO SOULS

Days passed. On her birthday, gaining confidence, he decided to propose her. He arrived at the birthday party and to his surprise, Sita introduced her fiancé to him. The wedding engagement was done at the same party. Vasu, being heart-broken, returned home. Sita spent more time with her fiancé. Gap fissured between Sita and Vasu. Vasu felt alone and decided to accept the abroad offer. He vacated his house and handed over the key to house owner. He left India without informing Sita.

One day, Sita got a call from her fiancé. He told her that he was in relationship with a girl. They brokeup due to some misunderstanding. Then only he agreed to marry Sita. But then, the fiance's ex-girlfriend whom he loved realised her mistake. They both shared their worries and agreed to married. He said sorry to Sita. Sita couldn't accept it. Her eyes filled with tears. She congratulated him and cut the call.

Sita found herself missing. She never faced such situation in her life. She thought of meeting Vasu to share her misery. Sita went to his house and didn't find him. When she enquired his house owner, She came to know that Vasu already left India. Sita felt bad on knowing this. She tried to call him many times. But there was no response as Vasu changed his mobile number. Sita gave her mobile number to house owner and requested to let her know if she came across any information about Vasu.

FOUR

IS THERE ANY BAR TO SHUT THE LOVE?

Two years passed. Sita got engaged with his family friend. She was giving away the invitation to her kith and kin. She invited Vasu's house owner and enquired about Vasu. The house owner said she didn't hear anything from him. Then Suddenly something struck her mind and asked Sita to wait. The house owner went in search of something. After few minutes, she came with a notebook in her hand covered with dust and dirt. She gave it to Sita and told her that she got that notebook from Vasu's room while renovating the house before handing over it to a new tenant. Sita took it and found that it was Vasu's personal diary. She returned home kept it aside without reading it.

Days passed. Sita was busy with her wedding processions. It was a day before her marriage. She was tired as she was a lone warrior taking care of all responsibilities. She came to her room and sat quietly. She was thinking whether she missed anyone to invite. Sita thought of Vasu, while thinking, Vasu's diary came across her eyesight. She took it and started reading.

The diary was full of love. Quotes, poems describing Vasu's love towards Sita. He had written each and every moment he enjoyed with her. Sita's heart melted while reading it. She continued reading. She understood how much he loved her. The last written page was on her birthday when he last met her.

" Hey Sita, Don't you understand my love? I don't know when I started loving you. But I am very sure that I never been close and affectionate to anyone before. I was afraid of losing your friendship on expressing my love. But, I don't want to keep it myself. Whatever it takes, I gonna propose you today in your birthday party."

Sita was able to feel his love and his disappointment and pain. She wept. At that time, groom came and asked her why she was sad. She explained everything to him. Groom understood her love feelings towards him. So he decided to stop the marriage by taking the blame on himself. Also he wished Sita for the best future. Sita thanked him.

FIVE

IN SEARCH OF LOVE

Sita decided to meet Vasu. She decided to go London where Vasu lived. She was waiting for visa. She remembered the happy days that she spent with Vasu and imagined meeting Vasu in London and getting married to him. Finally she got Visa to England. She was waiting eagerly for the day to go there.

There was a news flashing on TV about the spread of a new novel corona virus in China. She didn't care about it much as she already came across hearing those new kinds of viruses in that decade like Nipah, Zika which didn't widespread in the world.

She was happy as there was only two days left for her departure. Suddenly there came the news, England has stopped passenger air service across the world amidst the spread of COVID-19 virus. Neither immigration nor emigration was allowed till further official announcements. On listening the news, she was heart-broken. Soon, COVID-19 was declared as pandemic. She spent the lockdown with sweet memories they had.

SIX

HEART-BROKEN SOUL

After six months, COVID norms were relaxed. The air services began. That time she moved to her destination successfully. On reaching the regional head office of company where Vasu was working, she enquired about him. She got his address and happily went to meet him. On the way, she came across the following scenario.

Vasu was riding a motorcycle with a woman and a child. They were waiting for green signal. The child called him "Dad, go fast", " Dad, I want those toys".

On seeing this, Sita was shocked. She thought Vasu changed his mind and entered a new life. He got married and had a child. She couldn't bear the sorrow. She came back India without meeting Vasu. Sita didn't marry anyone as she was vexed on losing the beautiful love from Vasu. Nobody met her expectations. She decided to be single forever.

SEVEN

MEETING OF MERGED HEARTS

Years passed as time and tide wait for none. Sita grew old. She was attending the same marriage the old man Vasu attended. Both of them stared each other. They identified each other. They sat outside under the tree. Vasu asked about her family. Sita replied that she was single as she didn't marry anyone and explained what had happened. Vasu was shocked on hearing this. He started weeping inside. Sita asked about Vasu's family. Vasu replied as follows:

" When I came London, I lived in a flat, where my neighbour Elizabeth lived with her only child Mercy. Mercy's father passed away unfortunately when she was too little to understand that. She used to call me daddy and played with me happily. I accompany Elizabeth and her child for shopping and we used to go picnic on weekends. Days passed, Elizabeth developed feelings towards me. She proposed me. I explained her about my past love and I convinced Elizabeth and made her married to a good man, Michael. I didn't marry anyone. I am a single old man. I came here for attending the marriage of Elizabeth's daughter Mercy.

Sita was shocked on hearing that from Vasu. Both realised their misunderstandings but time has reaped their youth.

Yet, Love has no limits, Love is not time's fool.

Finally, they proposed each other and shared their love.

"Love may be distracted but cannot be destroyed"

Printed by Libri Plureos GmbH in Hamburg, Germany

9 798888 059098